Jessy Runs Away

Rachel Anderson
and Shelagh McNicholas

Young Lions

Published in Young Lions 1989
Fifth impression March 1991

Young Lions is an imprint of
the Children's Division, part of
HarperCollins Publishers Ltd,
77–85 Fulham Palace Road, London W6 8JB

Text copyright © 1988 Rachel Anderson
Illustrations copyright © 1988 by Shelagh McNicholas

Printed and bound in Great Britain by
HarperCollins Manufacturing, Glasgow

Jessy watched her family getting
ready. She knew what it meant.
Her mum, her dad, and her sister
Anna were going out shopping.

Jessy watched her dad put his coat
on and find the car keys.

He was ready to go.

So was Anna.

But Jessy knew
that she was going
to have to stay
behind with
Mrs Dawkins and
do jig-saw puzzles.

4

Mum was nearly ready too.
'Just got to find my list,' she said.

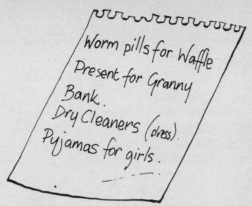

Now you'll be a good girl with
Mrs Dawkins, won't you Jessy?'

Jessy wanted to go with them.

'Shopping,' she said.

She liked Mrs Dawkins. But she liked going into town even better.

She liked seeing the colours of things in the windows, and the hurrying people, and the cars rushing by, and the chocolate biscuits in the supermarket. She liked going to the cafe where Mrs Dawkins' daughter worked.

Most of all, she just liked being out
and about with her family.

Even though Jessy was older than
her sister she didn't know or
understand as many things as
Anna did. And even the things
Jessy did know, she couldn't
remember for long.

'Come on Waffle,'
said Anna, and
she fixed Waffle's
lead on to his
collar.

'Soon as they're out of the way, we'll do a nice puzzle together,' said Mrs Dawkins kindly. But Jessy tugged anxiously at her coat on its hook.

Jessy nodded. Sometimes Jessy couldn't talk very well and people didn't understand her. But Anna always understood. Jessy loved her little sister Anna who always tried to take care of her.

No Jessy. Not today darling. Another time maybe.

Oh Mum! Why not? You know she loves coming out.

Because we've got such a lot to get done. Jessy only holds us up. Remember what happened last time? It's so tiresome when she runs away.

'Poor Jessy,' said Anna. She often felt sad when her sister couldn't join in with things like other children. 'She ought at least to be allowed to help choose her own pyjamas. She might not like a colour we chose and she'd be stuck with them forever.'

'Well,' said Mum slowly. 'Oh, all right. But listen, Jessy, you've got to keep near me and Dad all the time. And promise, promise, promise not to run away. You wouldn't want to go getting lost, would you now?'

Jessy shook her head.

All the way to
town, Jessy sat
quiet as a kitten,
being as good as
she could.

There was a lot of traffic about.

They had to drive

right up to the top

of the multi-storey
car park

before they found
an empty space.

Anna undid Jessy's seat-belt for
her and they both scrambled out.

Jessy took hold of Waffle's lead and
tried to pull him out too.

'No Jessy,' said Mum. 'It's too
crowded for Waffle in the shops. We
must leave him here. He'll mind the
car for us.'

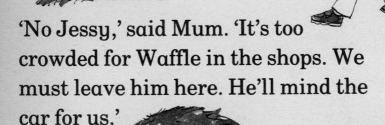

First they went to the bank.

Then they went to the dry-cleaners.

After that, they went to the gift
shop to buy a present for Granny.

Jessy knew exactly
what to choose. It was
a lamp shaped like a
Spanish dancer.

'My oh my, she'll just love that!'
said Dad.
'Course she will,' said Anna.
'Granny likes everything Jessy does.'
'Yes,' said Jessy. 'For Granny.'
Jessy was helpful
and carried
the parcel.

Next they went to get Waffle's worm pills. In the pet shop, Jessy tested some dog mix and talked to a parrot in a cage.

By now, they were all feeling tired.

'Time for a sit down,' said Mum, so they went to the cafe where Mrs Dawkins' daughter, Rose, worked.

'Food!' said Jessy. Food was one of Jessy's favourite things.

'Hello, and how's my best pal Jessy
today?' Rose said.
Jessy made a mess with her
fizzy drink.
'Never mind, Jessy pal,' said Rose.
'I'll clean up after you.'

The shops were even more crowded
now.

Phew, nearly through,
thank goodness.

What about our pyjamas?
I thought we were
going to get them first?

They went to the big store to buy
the pyjamas last of all.

Second
Floor .
Children's Wear .
Evening Wear .
Ladies Shoes .

Restaurant 3rd Floor

They had to find the right
department for Children's
Nightwear. But Jessy didn't want
pyjamas any more.

She saw a
lovely sparkling
evening dress.

'Let's just take your coat off for a
moment, Jessy, while we try this
one for size,' said Mum.

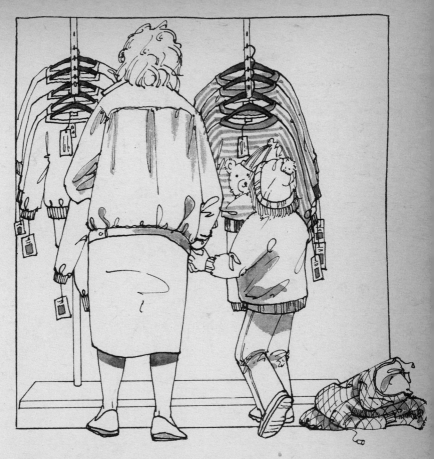

The pyjamas were nice. Jessy liked
them, except she wanted blue,
not pink.
'Blue please,' she said. 'Yes, blue.'
'Wait a moment then,' said Mum.
'Let's see if they've got your size
in blue.'

Jessy could still see the lovely sparkling dress on the other side of the shop.

She wanted to go and touch it. So she let go of Mum's hand

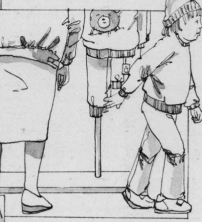

and got behind a rack of coats

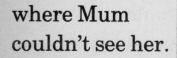

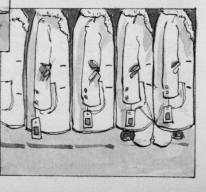

where Mum couldn't see her.

It was like playing hide-and-seek.
Jessy could see Mum, but Mum
couldn't see her.

Jessy watched Mum search
around for her, then come over to
the rack of coats. Jessy snuggled
herself in more deeply so that Mum
couldn't see her at all.

But it was too dark and too scary to stay in there for long. So Jessy came out and went back to the pyjama place.

But she couldn't see Mum there any more.

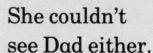

She couldn't see Dad either.

Nor Anna.

Jessy felt angry.
'I'm me!' she said crossly.
'Jessy's here!'
They shouldn't have gone without her.

'All right, all right,' she said to herself. If they hadn't waited for her to come out from behind the coats, she wouldn't wait for them. She would go and have a nice time without them.

'Have a nice day,' she said to herself, and with a

skip and a hop

Jessy was out of the shop.

There were lots of good things to see
outside. She saw a man collecting
money in a rattly tin, and she saw a
dog tied to a dog-rail waiting for its
owner, and she saw a fish shop

and she saw a shop full of
wheelbarrows. And then, over on
the other side of the road, she saw a
shop that looked as though it was
full of chocolate . . .

Jessy went with all the other busy people across the road.

But the shop on the other side wasn't a chocolate shop after all. So Jessy waited by the kerb to go across the road again.

A huge bus came along.
Then a lorry, so fast it
nearly knocked her over.
Then another bus and
three cars.

Jessy wanted to go back across the road.

She must get back to the other side.

She tried again. But there was so much traffic.

A driver wound down his window and shouted at her.

Jessy opened her mouth and screamed. When she screamed like that at school, Miss King always came running. Nobody at school liked it when she screamed. But at least they noticed. Today, nobody noticed her. Everybody was more interested in the shops.

Jessy thought about the car waiting in the multi-storey car park. Jessy thought how warm and safe it was sitting inside her car.
But where was the car?

Waffle was minding the car. Jessy wished she was with Waffle now.

She thought, I am all alone.

She was cold, she was frightened
and she was beginning to get wet.

Jessy began to run this way and
that way, up and down the busy
pavement.

Jessy thought, will they find
me here?

Jessy thought, will they want to
find me here?

Jessy thought, how will they
find me?

Suddenly,
   she saw a man
     on the other side of
      the road. It was her
      Dad looking for her.
      She was sure it
      must be Dad.

Jessy waved to him.
He saw her but didn't
wave back. Perhaps it
wasn't her dad after all.

A boy put out
his tongue,

and a pushchair
wheeled over
one of her feet,

a woman with spiky heels trod on the other.

People shoved. People pushed. But nobody took any notice of Jessy.

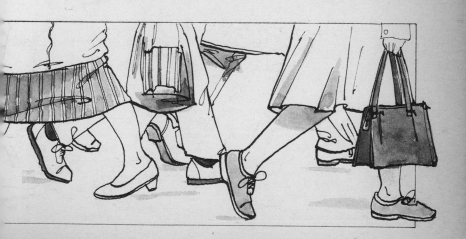

She saw a woman with a nice face.

'Mum? Find Mum. Here's Jessy,'
she said and she put her hand out.

But the woman stared at her and hurried away, tippy-tappy with her full shopping bags.

Jessy wanted to be good. Jessy wanted to be better than she had ever been before. But it's hard to know how to be good when you're on your own because you've run away and got yourself lost.

Then Jessy thought of two good things she must do. First she decided not to run back across the road even though she wanted to be over the other side.

The second good thing she decided
to do was to stop rushing about, and
to stand quite still.

As soon as she began to stand still,
she saw something that she knew
she had seen before.

It was the cafe though it didn't look quite the same as before. There were no cakes in the window any more.

There were no people sitting inside,
and most of the lights inside were off.
It looked so different that Jessy
wondered if it was the same cafe.

She looked in through the window.
Mum wasn't there. Dad wasn't
there. Anna wasn't there either.
The chairs were piled
up on the tables and
the waitresses were
washing the floor.
They were getting
ready to close the cafe
for the end of the day.

One of the waitresses saw Jessy and came to the door.

Hi there.

Find Mum.

Aren't you Rose's little friend? 'Fraid she's gone already.

Jessy. Ten.

Ten years old are you? Ooh that's nice.

No no no

'No, no,' said Jessy. She wanted to say she lived at Number Ten. But Number Ten What? Anna knew their address. Anna had tried to help Jessy learn it. If only Anna were here now. Anna could always make people understand.

Jessy shook her head. She certainly
did not want to be lost.

Never mind. I'll look it up in the book.

What's your surname?

Jessy. Find my mum.

Look inside her hat. Maybe she's got her surname in there.

Jessy took off her bobble hat and they found the name-tape sewn inside. This had Jessy's name.

J. Woodall

'Oh good!' said one of the girls. 'Now we can look up your telephone number in the book. Then we can telephone your home, and tell your family you're here and you're all right.'

One of the girls went off to telephone. She was back quite quickly.

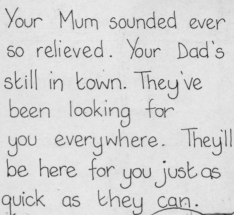

Your Mum sounded ever so relieved. Your Dad's still in town. They've been looking for you everywhere. They'll be here for you just as quick as they can. Won't be long dear!

But it seemed to Jessy to be a very long wait. The girls were kind to Jessy. They made her a cup of tea and asked her if she'd like a bun but she didn't want anything.
She felt bad.

At last, Mum and Dad arrived. Jessy was glad to see them again. But they didn't seem very pleased to see her.

'My goodness, we've been worried sick about you!' said Mum crossly. Dad looked cross too. Only Anna wasn't cross. She rushed straight over to Jessy and hugged her hard.

Jessy's mum and dad thanked the girls in the cafe for looking after Jessy. But driving home in the car everybody was very quiet.

Mrs Dawkins was waiting on the
doorstep with Waffle. Jessy was
glad to see her dear home again.
But she felt too ashamed to get out
of the car.

'Come along now, Jess,' said her
dad. But he didn't smile at all. Jessy
knew he was very annoyed with her.

Jessy crept in and sat
in the corner of the
room trying to be as
small as a mole in a hole.

Anna jumped up and down and tried
to cheer her up.

Can we have tea by
the fire to celebrate?
And afterwards wrap
up Granny's present?
And try on the new
clothes? And Jessy too?

Jessy has been a bold girl and caused a great many people an awful lot of worry. People who behave like that can't expect treats all the time can they?

I think Jess knows that, don't you?

Jessy felt very sad inside. She nodded. She knew she'd made a good day out into a bad day out.

But she was a bit sensible too, wasn't she? She was good making sure she didn't get quite lost. Bet you had to think really hard for that didn't you Jessy?

Jessy smiled. She was glad she had a sister like Anna who understood about things. She was glad she had a mum and a dad who loved her enough to come looking for her.

Not run away again. Not ever, ever!

**Dad made up the fire.
Mum got the tea ready.**

There's my girl!

We're all very glad you're safe and sound again

And when Jessy sat by the fire with Anna, she knew how lucky she was to be back with her family.